So You Want
to Be a Witch?

If the world tells you that you cannot "be," create a new one and leave a door open for others to follow.

So You Want to Be a Witch?

ISBN: 979-8-9865649-0-6

Copyright © 2022 by W.B. Clark

www.wbclarkbooks.com

So You
Want to
Be a
Witch?

Story &
Pictures by
W.B. Clark

"So, you want to be a witch?"

"Well, there is no room for someone like you."

Academy of Witchcraft

"Don't give up!"

"I can show you
how to be
a witch."

"Admire the flowers."

"Be nice to spiders."

"Hunt for treasure."

"Go with the wind."

"Sing to the trees."

"But most of all,

Murielle's Room

to be a witch..."

"Because you
are enough."